Also by Beth Bacon

I Hate Reading

THE BOOK
NO ONE
WANTS TO
READ

by Beth Bacon

PUSHKIN CHILDREN'S

Pushkin Press
71–75 Shelton Street
London WC2H 9JQ

The Book No One Wants to Read was originally self-published by Pixel Titles in 2017

The Book No One Wants to Read was first published by HarperCollins US in 2021

First published by Pushkin Press in 2021

1 3 5 7 9 8 6 4 2

ISBN 13: 978-1-78269-319-2

Design by Headquarters (Corianton Hale & Jason Grube)
www.hqtrs.com

Printed and bound in Italy by Printer Trento SRL

www.pushkinpress.com

To the students and staff
at Miramar Ranch Elementary

How about that!
You picked me up!

HOO!

Someone actually wants to read me.

I've been waiting for ages for someone like you to choose me.

Are you ready to get started?

LET'S GO!

Wait—*what?*

WHY
ARE YOU
LOOKING
AT ME LIKE
THAT?

I'VE SEEN THAT LOOK BEFORE.

You're not one of those kids who thinks books are boring, are you?

OH.
I GET IT.

You only picked me up
because you had to.

YOU'D RATHER BE

SOMEWHERE ELSE

ANYWHERE ELSE

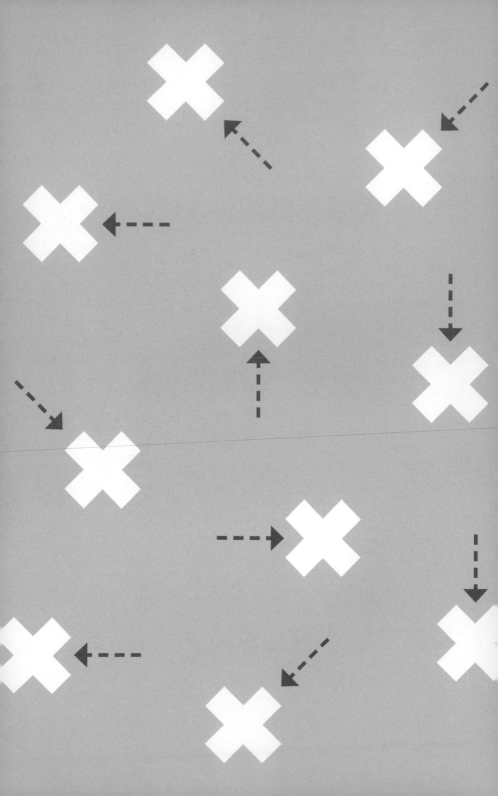

EVERYWHERE ELSE.

If you think reading is boring, try sitting around all day facing the wall, cover closed, doing a whole lot of *nothing*.

Hey,
I might
have an idea
that helps us
both.

WHAT IF...

YOU

sit here and turn
my pages, and...

WE

just goof off?

Everyone will think you're reading.

And I get a little time off the shelf.

I WON'T TELL ANYONE IF YOU WON'T.

Are you in?

Let's shake on it.

WAIT, I DON'T HAVE HANDS.

Well, just

me anyway.

Yeah! That's what
I'm talking about.

NOW...

Do you like
scratch and sniff?

SCRATCH HERE.

Smells like paper, huh?

WHAT DID YOU EXPECT?

Now try this:

SCRATCH
HERE.

Stinky, right?

GOTCHA!

Still paper.

HEY, DON'T CLOSE ME!

I'm just having
a little fun.

Give me
another chance.

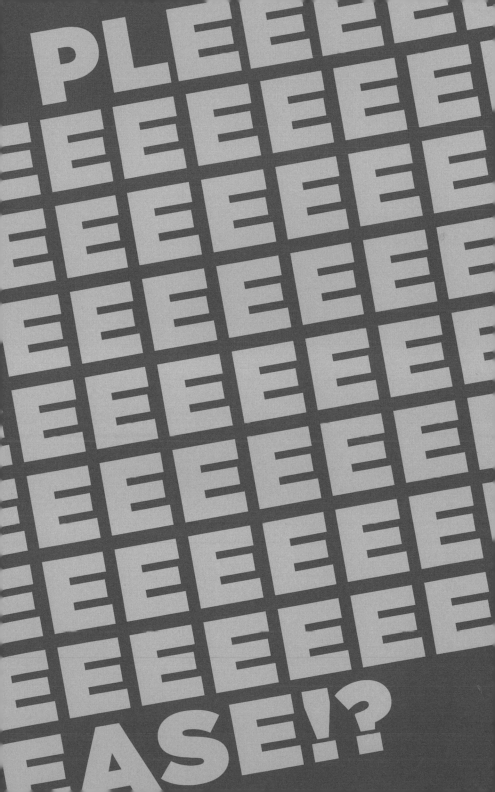

Let's play my
favourite game.

ROCK

PAPER

SCISSORS

We each think of one of these things:

ROCK

PAPER

SCISSORS

When I say,

"GO"

we both say what
we're thinking.

Here's how we tell
who wins:

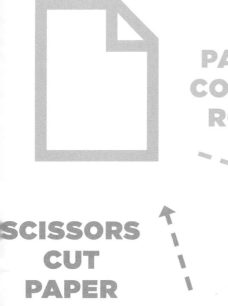

PAPER
COVERS
ROCK

SCISSORS
CUT
PAPER

ROCK
SMASHES
SCISSORS

Ready?

GO!

PAPER!

Did I win? HA!
Let's try again.

PAPER!

GOTCHA!

Wait, you got me?

Can you read
my mind?

Nevermind.

GO!

PAPER!

Wow, you won again?
You're too good!

Let's try
something else.

BLINK.

How about

BLINK.

a staring contest.

BLINK.

GO!

You blinked!

I WIN.

(I don't have eyelids.)

Speaking of
eyelids, can you

WINK?

Close one eye.

Now try the next.

Why is one side

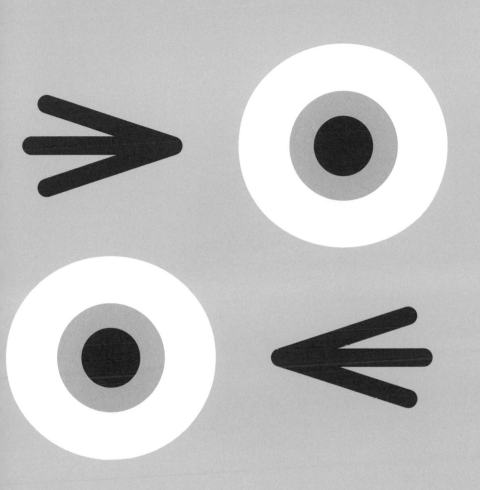

harder than the other?

Careful—don't close
both at the same time.

(Someone might think
you're not reading.)

Some kids can roll their tongue like a taco.

Can you?

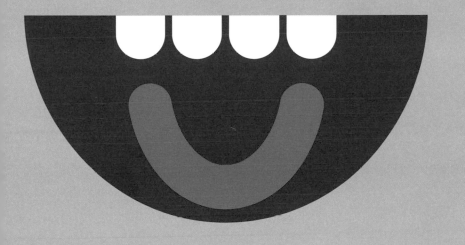

What about wiggling your ears?

Then try wiggling

your nose instead!

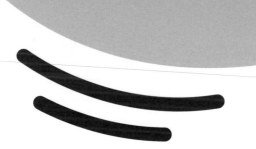

Now wiggle your bum.

But not too much!
(People will definitely think you're not reading.)

Try wiggling your ears

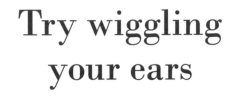

nose and bum
all together.

Now
wink

and
make a
tongue taco!

UH-OH!

Is someone looking?

QUICK!

Turn the page.

ding, reading, reading, reading, reading, read
, reading, reading, reading, reading, reading,
ding, reading, reading, reading, reading, read
, reading, reading, reading, reading, reading,
ding, reading, reading, reading, reading, read
, reading, reading, reading, reading, reading,
ding, reading, reading, reading, reading, read
, reading, reading, reading, reading, reading,
ding, reading, reading, reading, reading, read
, read   ing,
ding,   **PRETEND YOU'RE** read
, read   **READING.**   ing,
ling,   read
, reading, reading, reading, reading, reading,
ling, reading, reading, reading, reading, read
, reading, reading, reading, reading, reading,
ling, reading, reading, reading, reading, read
reading, reading, reading, needing, reading,
ling, reading, reading, reading, reading, read
reading, reading, reading, reading, reading,
ling, reading, reading, reading, reading, read
reading, reading, reading, reading, reading,
ling, needing, reading, reading, reading, read
, reading, reading, reading, reading, reading,
ling, reading, reading, reading, reading, read
reading, reading, reading, reading, reading,
ling, reading, reading, reading, reading, read

ding, reading, reading, reading, reading, read
, reading, reading, reading, reading, reading,
ding, reading, reading, reading, reading, read
, reading, reading, reading, reading, reading,
ding, reading, reading, reading, reading, read
, reading, reading, reading, reading, reading,
ding, reading, reading, reading, reading, read
, reading, needing, reading, reading, reading,
ding, reading, reading, reading, reading, read
, reading, reading, reading, reading, reading,
ding, reading, reading, reading, reading, read
, reading, reading, reading, reading, reading,
ding, reading, reading, reading, reading, read
, reading, reading, reading, reading, reading,
ding, **SQUINT. NOD.** ing, read
, read **TILT YOUR** reading,
ding, **HEAD.** ing, read
, read reading,
ding, reading, reading, reading, reading, read
, reading, reading, reading, reading, reading,
ding, reading, reading, reading, reading, read
, reading, reading, reading, reading, reading,
ding, reading, reading, reading, reading, read
, reading, reading, reading, reading, reading,
ding, reading, reading, reading, reading, read
, reading, reading, reading, reading, reading,
ding, reading, reading, reading, reading, read

You might want to bookmark that last page so you can flip there whenever someone checks to see if you're reading.

IT'S SURE TO FOOL THEM.

Oh, and some of the words back there don't say "reading." Bet you can't find them.

Let me know if you are **NEEDING** help.

(Psst. There are three.)

Follow the maze
to the ✖ with
your finger.

OH, THAT
TICKLES!

What do mazes have
to do with reading?

NOTHING!

But when some kids
read, they drag their
finger under the
sentence.

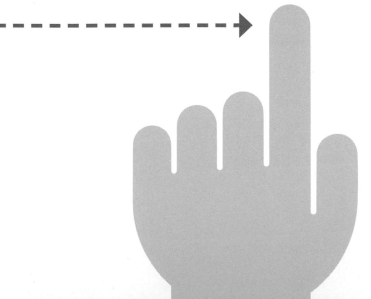

It's like they have
an eye at the end
of their finger.

WHAT IF
THEY DID?

Every time they point,
they'd poke themselves in the eye!

OUCH!

Hey, I have a joke.

Want to hear it?

What's the tallest building in the world?

A library, because it has so many stories!

Not funny? Geez. Tough crowd.

Here's another.

Did you hear about
the anti-gravity book?

IT'S
IMPOSSIBLE
TO PUT DOWN.

That one's my favourite.

Do you think it's about me?

MAYBE IT IS,
BECAUSE
YOU HAVEN'T
PUT ME
DOWN.

THANKS, FRIEND!

I *can* call you friend now, right?

Friends help each other out, and that's what we're doing.

IT SURE FEELS GOOD TO HAVE A FRIEND!

Do you like puzzles?
I do. Here's one:

Try to get the red
glass off the tray.

Stumped?
Flip me upside
down!

Flip me again!

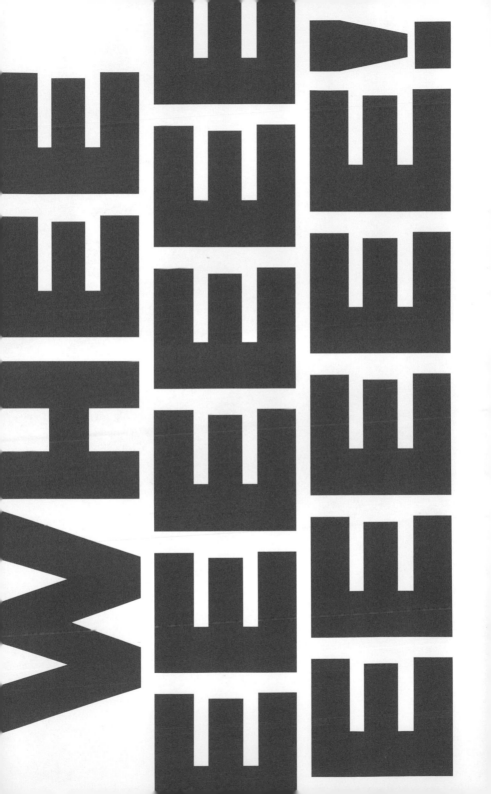

HOA!

I think I'm gonna...
I'm gonna...

Just give me a
minute

till everything
stops spinning.

Just pretend
you're reading.

1 - - - - Hold still - - - - → **2**

and move ← **3**

3 - - - - your eyes - - - - → **4**

from dot ← **5**

5 - - - - to dot - - - - →

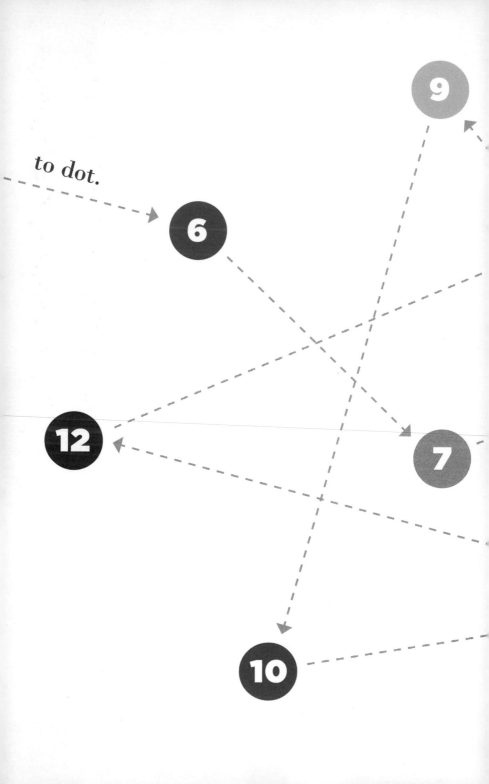
to dot.

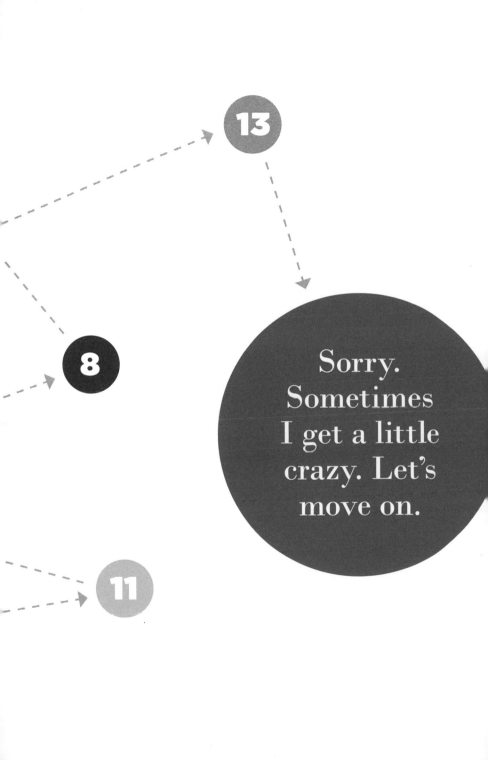

What do these

three phrases have

in common?

TACO CAT

YO BANANA BOY

TOO BAD I HID A BOOT

Each one is spelt

the same backwards

as forwards.

TACO CAT

YO BANANA BOY

TOO BAD I HID A BOOT

(Even in a mirror.)

Which **BLUE LINE** is longer?

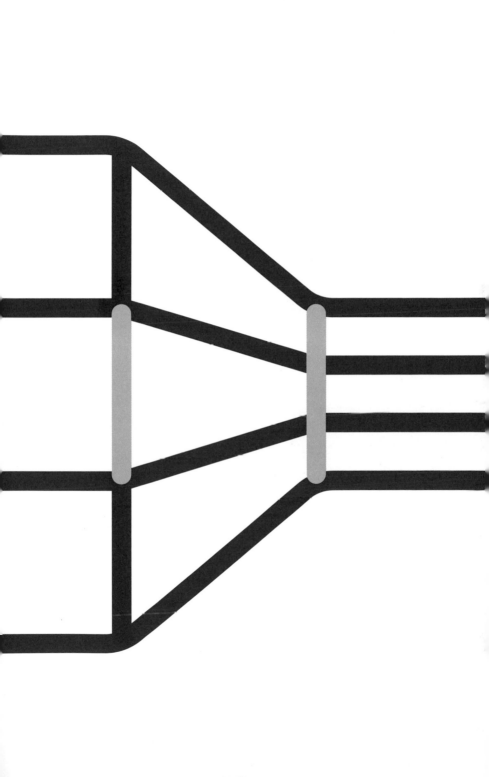

Tricked you.
They're the same.

What about these
two black dots?

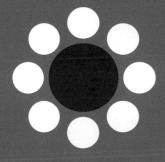

Which one is bigger?

Yup.

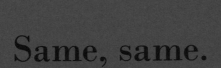

Same, same.

What if I told you

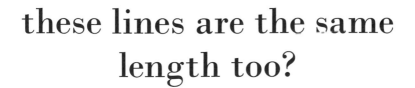

these lines are the same
length too?

You got me.

Sometimes I stretch the truth.

Speaking of
stretching, my
spine could use
a little

TCH

AAAAAAAAA

AAAAAAAAAAH!

Now that was
relaxing.

YAWN.

You're not yawning too,
are you?

Wow, it looks like I'm coming to an end.

Anytime you want to hang out, I'll be right where you left me.

HMM...

You look kinda
bummed out.

Not *that* kind of bum.

(Sheesh.)

Don't worry about me. I'll feel good going back on the shelf knowing I have a pal.

If you don't want to stop, you can always go back to page

OK.
C-YA!

HIGH
5

Oh, I forgot again.
I don't have hands, so

JUST SMACK ME HERE.

OUCH!

Just kidding!

(Didn't hurt.)